Kathrin Schärer

How Do You Feel?

Kane Miller
A DIVISION OF EDC PUBLISHING

feeling curious

feeling anxious

feeling happy

feeling sad

feeling guilty

feeling offended

feeling anticipation

feeling contented

feeling alone

feeling connected

feeling apprehensive

feeling triumphant

feeling comforted

feeling queasy

feeling brave

feeling bored

feeling unique

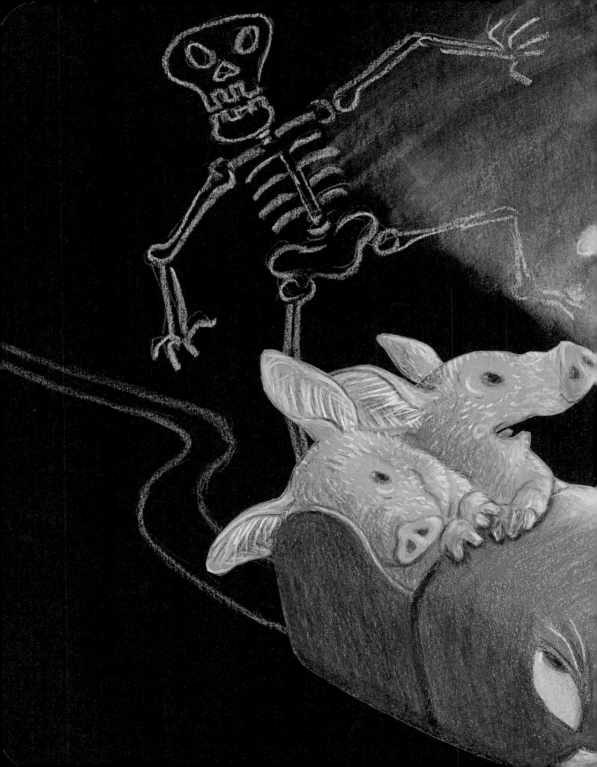

feeling scared

feeling playful

feeling protected

feeling impatient

feeling undecided

feeling
annoyed

feeling excluded

feeling furious

feeling touched

feeling shy

feeling safe

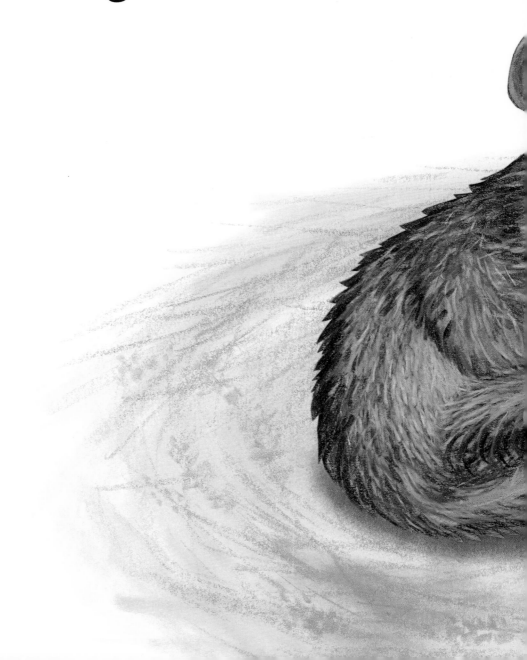

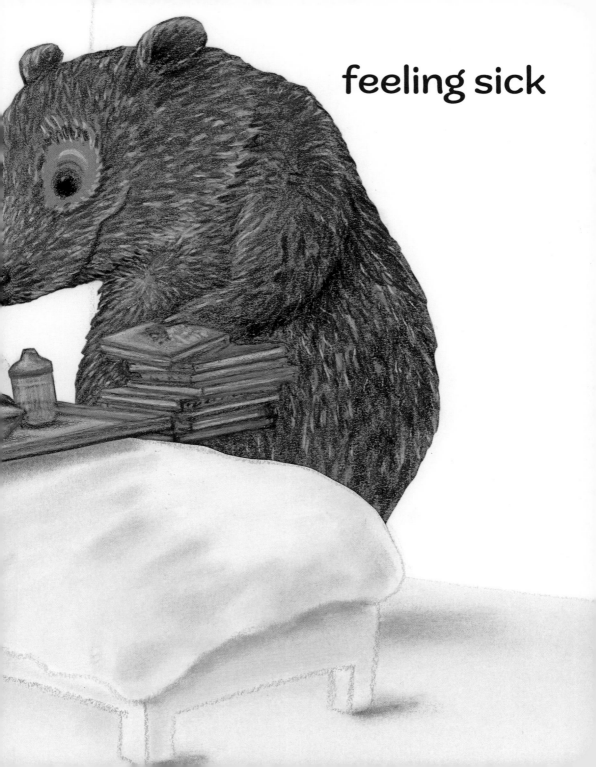

feeling sick

feeling lost in another world

feeling everything

für Hanspeter

Kathrin Schärer was born in Switzerland in 1969, and has illustrated numerous award-winning books for children.

First American Edition 2023
Kane Miller, A Division of EDC Publishing

By Kathrin Schärer
© 2021 Carl Hanser Verlag GmbH & Co. KG, München
First published in Germany in 2021 by Carl Hanser Verlag GmbH & Co. KG, München.

For information contact:
Kane Miller, A Division of EDC Publishing
5402 S 122nd E Ave, Tulsa, OK 74146
www.kanemiller.com

Library of Congress Control Number: 2022943748

Manufactured by Regent Publishing Services, Hong Kong, China
Printed November 2022 in Shenzhen, Guangdong, China
1 2 3 4 5 6 7 8 9 10

ISBN: 978-1-68464-697-5

FSC
www.fsc.org
MIX
Paper | Supporting
responsible forestry
FSC® C013314